My m Book

by Jane Belk Moncure

illustrated by Linda Hohag

THE CHILD'S WORLD

ELGIN, ILLINOIS 60120

Library of Congress Cataloging in Publication Data

Moncure, Jane Belk.
  My "m" book.

  (My first steps to reading)
  Rev. ed. of: My m sound box. © 1979.
  Summary: Little m finds things beginning with the
letter m to put in his box, including a magician who
takes them all to the moon.
  1. Children's stories, American. [1. Alphabet]
I. Hohag, Linda. ill. II. Moncure, Jane Belk. My
m sound box. III. Title. IV. Series: Moncure, Jane
Belk. My first steps to reading.
PZ7.M739Mym 1984   [E]   84-17556
ISBN 0-89565-286-2

Distributed by Childrens Press, 1224 West Van Buren Street,
Chicago, Illinois 60607.

My "m" Book

Little m had a box.

It was a green box.

He said, "I will fill my  box."

Little m found

monkeys.

He put the monkeys into the box.

Little **m** found

one,

two,

three mice.

Then he found many more mice.

He put the mice into the box
with the monkeys.

But the monkeys did not like the mice.

The monkeys were mad.

They jumped out of the box

and ran...

up a mountain.

Little ⬛ ran. The mice ran too.

Then the monkeys ran
down the mountain.

The monkeys did not see
the mud.

They fell into the mud.

Now they were very mad.
What a mess.

Little  and the mice pulled the monkeys out of the mud.

Little  put the monkeys back into the box.

"Monkeys and mice, be nice," he said.

Little m

met a moose.

"Moose," he said, "you are just what I need for my mice."

Little  saw a merry-go-round.

"Let's go for a ride," he said.
He found money.

And they went for a ride
on the merry-go-round.

Little  looked up.

Guess what he saw?

 The moon.

"The moon belongs in my box," he said.

"How can I get to the moon?"

Just then,

Little  m met a
magician.

"I will take you to the moon

in my

magic
moon machine,"

said the magician.

And he did.
He took them to the moon.

magic
moon
machine

monkey

moon

mouse

mouse

mouse

Some magic!

magician

monkey

moose

mouse

monkey

27

More words with Little

mittens

magnet

marbles

mop

milk

moccasins

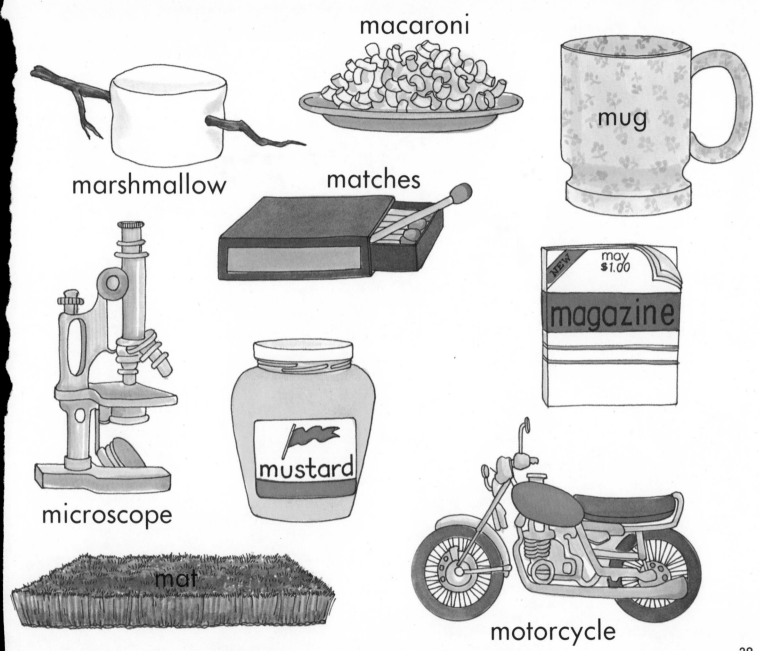

marshmallow

macaroni

matches

mug

microscope

mustard

magazine

mat

motorcycle

29